Waira's First Journey

EUSEBIO TOPOOCO

Waira's First Journey

LOTHROP, LEE & SHEPARD BOOKS   NEW YORK

It is summer in the country of the Aymara Indians. Tall mountains covered with yellowish grass shimmer against the azure sky. It is the middle of the day, and the sun is burning.

On the slope of the mountain Tiwanaku, a small Aymara family is resting. They have been traveling for five days. Waira and her mother, Khenamaya, sit down. Her father, Shaska, tends to the llamas. Hungry and thirsty, they hurry to the thorny bushes with the yellow flowers. Their leaves are the llamas' favorite food.

This is Waira's first long journey. She and her parents are on their way to the market in Topojo, and there is much to see along the way.

"Look there," says Mother, "down in the valley. Those are the ruins of Tiwanaku, the city that our ancestors built long, long ago. There they used to gather from all around, several times a year, to thank Father Sun and Mother Earth for their good crops."

Waira's eyes glow as she imagines Tiwanaku seething with life again. Then something else catches her eye. "What is that bird?" she asks, pointing to the sky.

"It is the condor," Mother answers, "the ruler of the Andes. In it dwell the spirits of our forefathers." The big bird flies higher and higher, farther and farther away. Soon it is no more than a black spot in the sky. "The condor is free, Waira," Mother continues. "It has always been free. Once we were as free as it is."

When Father returns with the llamas, the family walks down to the ancient city. Soon they stand in front of a large and wide gate. Through its entrance, the sun is shining.

"This is the Sun Gate," Mother explains. She lifts Waira up to see the suns and condors carved into the wall. "The carvings represent the months of the year."

Then they walk to another gate. This one lies tumbled on the field. Waira's mother lays her hand on it.

"And this is the Moon Gate," she says. "It is the largest gate of Tiwanaku, and it was made of one single piece of stone. When I was a small child, my father told me that it weighs hundreds of thousands of kilos."

"What happened to the city?" asks Waira.

Mother points at a huge mountain in the distance.

"That mountain is a volcano," she says. "A long, long time ago, there was a terrible eruption. The earth trembled. The waters of Lake Titicaca rose. Enormous waves washed over the city and drowned it. Hundreds of years passed before the water withdrew."

"Did all the people drown, too?"

"No," says Mother, "many people survived. But after the catastrophe, the climate turned colder. Many people left in search of warmer places. Only some of them remained." Mother Khenamaya grows silent. Her eyes glow as she watches her daughter.

"Those people who stayed," Waira asks, "they are us?"

Mother nods. Then she smiles as broadly as Waira. "Yes, they are us."

They continue their journey, stopping again only when they reach a house by Lake Titicaca. Here, the year's first crop of maize has been spread on a layer of leaves for the sun and the wind to dry the cobs.

There are red, yellow, and brown cobs. Waira likes the red and yellow ones best. Red maize can be ground and mixed with warm water and sugar to make a fine drink on a cold day. And Waira herself has roasted yellow maize in a clay pot. The roasted kernels make a good snack.

Father and Waira walk toward the family living in the house.

"Brother, we have come to visit you," says Father.

The man rises before answering. "How nice," he says.

"You are most welcome." They chat for a little while, then Father fetches the llamas and unloads them.

"We bring with us wool, dried potatoes, and both fresh and dried meat," he tells the man. "We would like to barter them for dried fish, maize, and vegetables."

The man nods. "With pleasure," he answers.

Waira and the boy of the house watch their fathers barter.

"Your father is strange," says the boy. "He said he had fresh meat to barter, but he has not shown it. You have traveled a long way. Surely by now the meat must be rotten."

Waira starts to laugh. "No," she says, "the meat is still fresh. It walked here on its own."

The boy does not understand. He stares at Waira, amazed, but does not say anything.

Finally Waira points to the llamas. "There is the fresh meat," she says. "It is better to let it walk here by itself than to slaughter it at home and make the other llamas carry it."

Now the boy understands and smiles. "Your father is wise," he says.

"Yes," Waira agrees. "But it was my mother who taught him."

"My name is Sushi," says the boy. "What is yours?"

"Waira," answers Waira, and smiles. She likes this new friend very much.

"Tell me, Waira," says Sushi, "you have been traveling many days. Are you not tired from all that walking?"

"I did not walk the whole way," Waira tells him. "When I felt tired, I rode on my llama."

"Oh, how lucky you are!" says Sushi. "I have wanted a llama for a long time, but I do not have one yet."

Suddenly Waira has an idea. "Come," she says, and she leads Sushi to the llamas. She quickly gets hold of her black llama and brings it to Sushi. "You can have this one," she tells him.

Sushi stares at her as if he cannot believe what he has just heard. "But, Waira," he says, "then you will have no llama to ride when you are tired."

Waira smiles. She points to a reddish-brown llama nearby. "Do not worry," she says. "I still have that one. But you must promise me one thing, Sushi."

"Anything," says Sushi.

"On this llama you shall come and visit me," she says. "Just head for the big blue mountain with the white snowpeak. The llama knows the way."

"I promise," says Sushi. His eyes glow with joy.

Sushi wants to give Waira a present too, but he doesn't know what. He has to think for a long time before he gets an idea. "I shall catch a fish for you!" he announces at last.

They run to the lake. There Sushi fastens a little net to a forked branch. Then he jumps into the lake and swims to and fro underwater, holding the net.

Waira catches glimpses of him under the water and she waits excitedly. Finally he comes to the surface for air. They look into the net, but it contains only a frog.

Sushi is disappointed, but Waira is pleased with the present. "Maybe it is a fish who has turned itself into a frog in order not to be eaten," she says.

Just then they hear someone calling from the house. It is dinnertime.

The children hurry back and join the others. Everyone sits on the soft llama rugs. Sushi's mother pours fish soup from a clay pot, and Waira's parents offer food too—a big bowl filled with boiled potatoes and meat.

Then, in the dim light of the tallow lamp, they sit talking for a long time.

It is late when they all go to bed. Waira's family are invited to sleep inside the house, but they prefer to sleep in the open. Father Shaska and Mother Khenamaya spread llama rugs on the ground, and they have blankets to cover themselves.

Waira looks up into the starry sky and thinks of all she has seen today—first the ancient city of Tiwanaku, and now the great Lake Titicaca. She thinks of Sushi swimming beneath the clear water of the lake and remembers the huge plants growing along the shore.

"Father," she asks, "what are those plants that grow by the lake?"

"That is totora," Father tells her. "It has always been used for making the beautiful rush boats. Shall I tell you the story?"

"Yes, please," whispers Waira.

"Once, a very long time ago," Father Shaska begins, "a most unusual man lived on the shores of Lake Titicaca. Everyone thought he was very strange, for he never went hunting with the others. Instead, he spent his days by the lake, looking at the water. That is how he came to be known as Chaulla-Llaytha, Lazy Fish.

"Then one day Chaulla-Llaytha announced that he was going to build a rush boat big enough to sail far away, past the great mountains where the sun sets every evening. The others thought this was an excellent idea, and so they all set to work cutting totora, then setting it out to dry, and finally binding it together in large, strong bundles.

"At last the day came when the boat was finished and it was time to go. So they loaded it with supplies and sailed off to places no one had ever heard of before, exchanging knowledge with all the people they met on their way."

Waira sighs. "It must be fun to sleep on a boat," she whispers.

"I expect it is," says Father, but Waira is already asleep, with the field for her bed and the dark sky sparkling with stars for her roof.

The following morning Sushi is eager to show his father his new llama, so he and Waira go to fetch it. Waira also fetches the reddish-brown. Although she has not told Sushi, she is afraid that Father may be planning to barter her other llama. She wants to ride it one last time. She wants to show everyone how strong and swift it is.

Sushi's father admires his llama and feels its soft wool. "How beautiful it is," he says. "And llamas are so swift. When they run, their feet barely touch the ground."

Father Shaska clears his throat. "Brother," he says, "the reddish-brown llama is the fresh meat I brought." Waira holds her breath. "I had thought to slaughter it for you, but now Waira will need it for riding."

When Waira hears what her father is saying, she is so happy that she leaps onto the reddish-brown. Sushi's father helps him onto the black, and together they ride to the flock of llamas and drive it toward the house.

Then Sushi's father helps Shaska load the llamas. Soon they are finished.

Sushi's mother gives Waira a hug. "Sweet little Waira," she says, "I have been watching you. You are both clever and generous. We will always remember you."

Father Shaska and Mother Khenamaya smile proudly. Waira knows that they are pleased with her.

It is time to leave now. Father and Mother express their thanks. Then the family sets off in a neat little caravan. The llamas have rested and, despite their heavy burdens, they trip lightly over the grass-covered field. Waira's parents have selected twenty of the strongest llamas for this journey. They are all males; females are not used as pack animals because they often have young ones and so must stay at home.

After some days they reach a pleasant area called Khomanche. They stop there awhile to rest and let the animals drink. Waira remembers to fill her little leather sack with fresh water.

Then Father says, "Look, Waira, those cacti on the mountain are blooming. A cactus like that blooms only once every hundred years. If you see a flower, you will be granted a wish. But you must wish only for something that will benefit many people, not just yourself."

Finally they reach the market in Topojo. It is the day before the big fair, and from all directions Aymaras are arriving with their llama caravans. Some come from the high plains, others from the rain forest. Some of the families have walked for several days; others live only a single day's travel away. But all come here once a year to barter.

Waira is so tired by now, she can hardly stand up. Father finds a good place to camp. Waira watches as he unloads the llamas. "We still have dried potatoes and wool left," he says. "We can barter them for fruit and pottery and tools."

"Yes," says Mother, "and if we still need anything, we can barter some of our maize or dried fish."

Waira is very hungry. She finds three big stones and places them in a triangle. Then she collects twigs and dry llama droppings to make a fire. Finally she gathers a little dry grass and goes to a family whose fire is already burning. She lights her grass and hurries back to light her own fire with it.

Meanwhile, Father has built a wall of the llama sacks to protect the family against the wind which is blowing from the north. The field is wet from rain. Father gathers a lot of grass and spreads it on the campsite. Then Waira spreads the llama rugs on top of the grass and sits down at last. It is wonderful to rest after the long journey. Altogether pleased, she watches Mother prepare dinner. Tonight they are having boiled fish, vegetables, and potatoes.

After dinner Waira is no longer tired. She sits beside her mother, who has already fallen asleep. On her other side, Father is lying down too. All around them fires burn in the dark night. Musicians are playing, and Waira listens for a long time. Then she lies down to sleep too.

When Waira awakens, the sun has already risen.

"The soup is ready, Waira," says Mother.

The morning is filled with the sounds of drums and flutes. Waira can feel the festival in her whole body. She eats quickly, then dresses in her llamaskin dress and her prettiest ornaments.

"My beautiful little girl!" says Mother.

Father has taken the llamas to graze very early. When he returns, he must eat. Waira watches him impatiently. She waits until he has finished before she speaks.

"Could we go and have a look now?" she asks.

The market is filled with people dressed in gaudy costumes. There seem to be musicians everywhere. Waira is drawn to those who play the flute with one hand and the drum with the other. They dance as they play, and there are dancing condors, too.

"Oh, how beautiful!" says Waira.

Suddenly one of the condors dances right up to her and grabs her. "Now I've got you!" he shouts.

At first Waira is afraid. She hides behind her mother. But soon her fear passes and she pops out her head and shouts, "You won't catch me again! You are too old and tired!"

The condor laughs. "I am as quick as you," he says, "and I can dance and fly. Perhaps you have seen me in reality."

"Yes," says Waira, "in Tiwanaku."

"That was me on my way here," the man-condor jokes. "We condors are children of the sun. You too are a child of the sun. We all speak Aymará, do we not? We are born free, and free we will grow old, until one day, like the condor, we fly over the clouds of the Andes."

Waira is no longer afraid. "You speak beautifully, brother," she says. "I am happy to be an Aymara and to see you dance. I will tell my brothers and my grand-father what you have told me."

But the condor has not finished. "Long ago, our fore-fathers composed a tune for the condor," he says. "They played it on their reed pipes, and the condor came flying to them. Day and night they played for Father Sun and Mother Earth, and the condor danced and danced until it had lost all of its tail. In that way the condor gave its feathers to the Aymara. Since then we have used condor feathers for our headgear. Would you like one of mine?" And he puts a beautiful black-and-white feather in Waira's hair. Then he asks if she would like to dance with him.

"Oh, yes!" says Waira, and she dances and dances while Mother and Father watch, smiling.

But finally Mother calls, "Come now, Waira, we must go and barter."

Waira is very impressed by the market. There are fruits and vegetables, maize and other sorts of corn, llama skins and pottery, tools and wood. There are living foxes and pheasants and birds that speak Aymará. And everywhere, children are eating fruits and sweets and listening to the bargaining of the adults.

Mother leads Waira to a woman bartering pears. "Will you exchange your pears for dried potatoes?" she asks.

"Yes," says the woman, and she hands Waira a pear to taste. It is sweet and juicy and Waira is happy when Father lifts a whole sack onto his back. She and Mother and the pear woman walk to Waira's campsite together. There the woman gets her barter of dried potatoes.

After they have seen the whole market and bartered for everything they need, Father looks at the sun—it is already past midday. "It is time to go home," he says. And they load their sacks back onto the llamas and leave the market of Topojo.

They came to Topojo by a long route in order for Waira to see the ancient ruins of Tiwanaku. Now it takes them only two days to reach their home. In all, they will have walked for twelve days.

At last they reach Okhollani—home. The mild summer wind blows over them. The moon shines big and yellow, welcoming them. Waira's brothers come running. Grandfather happily waits in the doorway.

Waira feels warm and happy. What fun it will be to tell about Tiwanaku and the condor and all the sights of Topojo—and, best of all, about Sushi, who will one day come to visit, riding on Waira's black llama.

EUSEBIO TOPOOCO
Speaks About His Life

I was born in the land of the Aymara forty-seven years ago. My father was a chieftain, and I was the firstborn of his second marriage. We lived in the countryside, far south of Lake Titicaca in Bolivia. Our home was surrounded by moutains, dry in winter and productive in summer. We cultivated at least eight kinds of potatoes, each a different color.

At that time the Aymara people lived as dependents of Spanish landowners. We worked mostly for the landowners and only a little for ourselves. But we Aymaras stuck together. At age eight or nine, I began to help my parents make the colorful clothing that we wore to the annual festival, where all the Indians joined together to sing, play music, and dance.

When I was about sixteen, my father thought that I should go to school in La Paz so that I would be able to hold my own better than he against the land-owners. The school was taught in Spanish, which wasn't easy for me to learn since it is very different from Aymará. I attended evening classes and worked in a clothing shop during the day. After work I went to school, but I was very tired. Often I sat down behind the other forty or fifty students and slept, so I didn't learn much.

On the other hand, I now had a job and some money. Now and then films about the Vikings were shown in the local theater. I was so wild about them, I often watched the same film four times in one day. I thought that the Vikings had something in common with the Indians. They worshipped the sun just as we did.

When I arrived in Sweden twenty-two years ago, I could see in real life the people and the nature I had seen in films as a teenager in La Paz. Before I came to Sweden, I lived in Spain for a time, but the Spanish people didn't like me. I couldn't even get a cup of coffee in a cafe. I might have to wait half an hour for my coffee, and if I reminded the waiter of my order, he answered that I, an Indian, should be glad that the Spaniards taught me Spanish.

Before I began to paint, I worked on a Swedish farm, in a paper factory, and as an electrician. In my free time I read books in Swedish using a Swedish-Spanish

dictionary. There were an astonishing number of books about Indians, books that even today don't exist in Bolivia. When I wasn't reading, I made watercolor paintings of my childhood experiences.

In 1974 I had my first art exhibition in Sweden, and after several exhibitions I became a member of the Swedish National Association of Artists. Since then my sole occupation has been painting my experiences. My paintings have been well received in Sweden and also in France, Belgium, Germany, Norway, and Greenland, but not in Bolivia. The Bolivian authorities don't think paintings of "wild people" are worth having.

At my first exhibitions, each painting had a short description to go with it. That first gave me the idea to make a children's book. Also, I have for many years given talks about my people to both children and adults. My tales were greatly appreciated, and since there was no literature about the Aymara Indians, I felt a greater and greater need to depict the culture of my people in text and pictures. The result is *Waira's First Journey*. The original illustrations for the book were all painted in oil.

The Swedish language is difficult for me, and I often think in my own language, Aymará, or sometimes in Spanish, before I begin to write. But my imagination and my desire to tell about Aymara life help me to surmount the difficulties.

THE AYMARA INDIANS

There are about six million inhabitants of Bolivia. Of these, four million are Indians, over one million are Mestizos, and only about one hundred thousand are Creoles. The Aymara Indians are entirely self-sufficient. They live by cultivating the land and keeping cattle. But even though the Aymaras comprise the majority of the population, they have very little influence in their country. They are not even allowed to speak their own language, nor are they allowed to worship the Sun God, who is their god. If they do, they are labeled heathen and forced to become Christians.

The government is not particularly interested in having Aymara children attend school. If there are fewer than thirty children in a village, the government will not provide a teacher. When the children do have a teacher, they are taught only in Spanish, a language so different from Aymará that this is something like teaching American children all their lessons in Chinese. Because of this, the children don't learn much, and they learn nothing at all about their own history and culture.

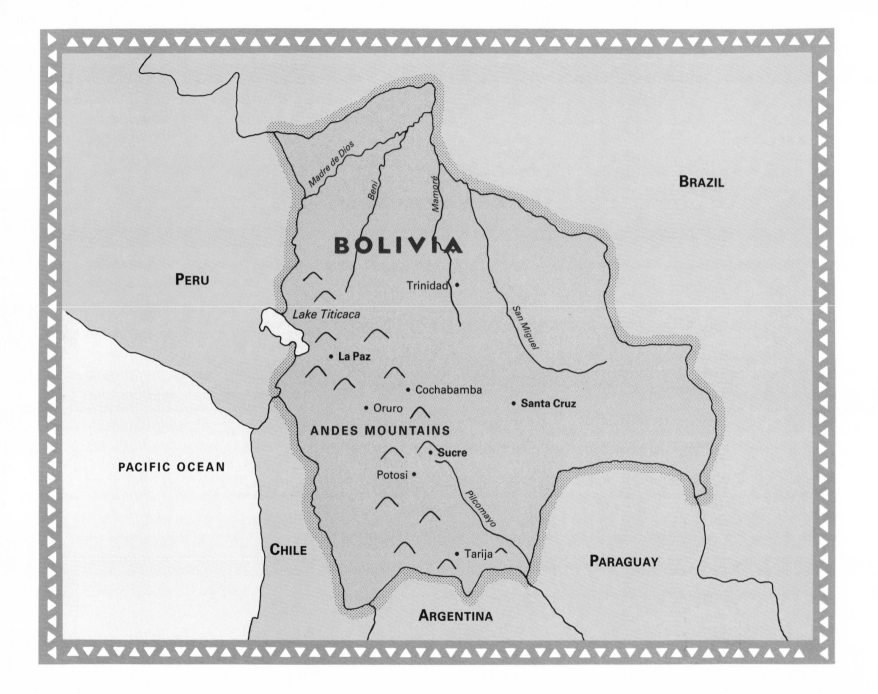

PERU

BRAZIL

Madre de Dios

Beni

Mamoré

BOLIVIA

Trinidad •

San Miguel

Lake Titicaca

• **La Paz**

• Cochabamba

• Oruro

• **Santa Cruz**

ANDES MOUNTAINS

• **Sucre**

Potosi •

Pilcomayo

PACIFIC OCEAN

CHILE

• Tarija

PARAGUAY

ARGENTINA

The Aymara Indians are descendants of a people who have existed for more than 25,000 years. The high point of their culture is sometimes called the Cradle of the Americas.

Long, long ago the Aymaras dressed like the people pictured in this book. They used llama hides for many purposes, including most of their clothing. But after the Spaniards conquered their land, the Aymaras were forced to wear Spanish clothing such as ponchos and hats. Only in a few distant areas and at festivals do some Aymaras still dress in their traditional clothing.

Today the majority of the Aymara people live in Khollasuyu, the country that was in 1925 named Bolivia. Bolivia is named for Simón Bolívar, the man who, thanks to help from the Indians, freed Bolivia from Spain. Unfortunately, only the Creoles (descendants of Spaniards) and Mestizos (descendants of Spaniards and Indians) are given credit for the country's independence, and it is they who rule the country today.

In this book, Waira lives in a place where the climate is both cold and dry, and so her family walks to warmer areas a couple of times a year to barter for the things they cannot grow at home. Waira's family lives in a traditional way, and they depend a great deal on their llamas. Llamas are so swift that when they run, their feet barely seem to touch the ground. But they are not

just beautiful. Without them, Waira's family would have difficulty managing. They make rugs and clothing from llama wool. They make rope from llama skin. And they eat llama meat.

Eusebio Topooco